MIDNIGHT
SNOWMAN

Mesquite Club
Charter Members
Memorial Endowment

Children's Literature
Collection

UNLV Library

1987-88

Joyce

Caroline Feller Bauer

MIDNIGHT SNOWMAN

illustrated by Catherine Stock

Atheneum 1987 New York

Atheneum. Macmillan Publishing Company, 866 Third Avenue, New York, NY 10022.
Type set by Fisher Composition, New York City. Printed and bound by Toppan Printing Company, Japan.
Typography by Mary Ahern. First Edition. 10 9 8 7 6 5 4 3 2 1

Library of Congress Cataloging-in-Publication Data

Bauer, Caroline Feller.   Midnight snowman.

SUMMARY: In a town where it hardly ever snows, one neighborhood's parents and children take advantage
of a late night snow by building a snowman before the snow turns to rain.
[1. Snow—Fiction] I. Stock, Catherine, ill.
II. Title. PZ7.B3258Mi   1987   [E]   86-26540
ISBN 0-689-31294-6

For Hilary and Elizabeth who built it (C.F.B.)

For Vanessa down under (C.S.)

It rains a lot in our town. It never snows. Last year Mr. Johnson read *The Snowy Day* to our class. I dreamed about making snow angels, and building a snowman.

Every winter morning, I look out the window before going downstairs to see if it has snowed.

Sometimes I have cream of wheat for breakfast. I make hills and valleys of snow in my dish until my mom sighs and says, "Finish your breakfast."

When I make my bed, I pretend that the top sheet is an Eskimo igloo. I am safe and warm inside, but outside I am surrounded by snow.

On the news there are often stories about blizzards in cities like Chicago. But it never snows where I live. It rains a lot in our town.

One Saturday night in January, I was playing with my dog Robbie. The phone rang. It was my friend Elizabeth. "Look out the window," she said.

It was snowing! The porch was covered with snow. The lawn was covered with snow. The street was covered with snow.

"Tomorrow I can make a snowman," I told my dad.

The phone rang again. This time Elizabeth had a great idea.

"Could we," I asked my parents. "Could we make a snowman, now, tonight?"

"Why not," my dad said. "The snow is probably perfect for packing."

By the time I'd found some mittens and a hat, it was ten o'clock.

Elizabeth and I went up to the Elman's house. They have a huge, flat lawn. We started with a small snowball and rolled it around and around the yard until it was much bigger.

"How will we get it back to your house?" Elizabeth asked.

"If we get it to the hill, we can roll it down," I said. The ball got larger and larger, heavier and heavier. We couldn't move it another inch.

"We need help," I said. "Peter used to live in Maine. I'll bet he's an expert at building snowmen."

Peter brought his little brother Aaron and
their dog Dunce.

"We need a shovel," Peter said. "Smirna has
one."

"But she's never seen snow in her life,"
Elizabeth said. "She just moved here from India
or someplace."

"So what," Peter said. "She has a shovel. She
can help."

Smirna came with her mother and father, who had never seen snow either. They were excited about our snowman too.

As we rolled the huge ball down the street, the Jensens and the Goldwaters came out to join us. Everyone had an opinion about just how a snowman should be built.

"This is going to be the biggest snowman in the world," I said.

The Rostows came home from a dinner party, woke
up their three kids, and joined our snow party too—
along with the babysitter.

We got to our yard, and my dad came out to tell us not to make such a racket. When he saw the crowd, he and his bridge partners decided to help. They had their opinions about the snowman too.

Soon it was midnight, the latest I'd ever been up. We had all worked hard and were finally done. I bet no one has ever built a nicer snowman. Well maybe he wasn't actually a snowman . . . maybe more of a snow *thing*. But then again, it rains a lot in our town. It hardly ever snows.

It is spring now. This morning I looked out the window and I thought "SNOW!", but it was just our cherry tree in bloom.